D1064220

You Are My Pride

A Love Letter from Your Motherland

Carole Boston Weatherford

Illustrated by E. B. Lewis

ASTRA YOUNG READERS

AN IMPRINT OF ASTRA BOOKS FOR YOUNG READERS

New York

I am the mother of all humanity.
I have a long history and a longer memory.
Most of all, I remember you,
my offspring of all colors
in all corners of the earth.
Let me remind you of our timeless bond.

Child, I knew you from the first—

when you were but a glimmer in some god's heart.

I held your soulful cells within me

before the sun ever kissed your skin,

before the wind blew breath into your lungs.

For ages, you stirred inside me yearning toward dawn.

Child, I stood at the brink of your evolution—
when you were without a yesterday
and all you had were tomorrows.

You were borne of my vast wilderness.
Child, I knew you before word or the drum,
before trade or tools, before fire or the hunt.
My caves sheltered you and my forests fed you.

Child, I cradled you when other creatures mocked your baldness, and I looked on amazed as you walked erect from the gorge.

Child, I knew you when your blood
teemed wild as the beasts',
and your feet were bare, and the earth
was your bed and the sun, your cloak.

Your trial then was to survive.

Child, I could not protect you from all dangers,
but I gave you a clever mind
to outwit swifter, stronger predators
and to weather fierce storms.

Child, you are mine as much as Mount Kilimanjaro,
as much as the Serengeti and the Sahara,
as much as the baobab and the bush.

I love the lion, the zebra, the gazelle, and the impala,
but you, child, are my pride.

I placed at your feet, the land and the sea.

And though you are my treasure,
I sent you around the globe, for I knew—
as well as I know you—that your gifts would shine.

Child, keep me in your heart,
and, like a long-ago song whose lyrics
are lost but whose melody lingers,

you will hear me whispering in a language
that belongs to no nation but to all humanity.

Here are your beginnings.

Here is your home.

Our Beginnings

Evolution traces change over time in life on Earth. Evolution explains the similarities among different life forms, the changes that occur within populations, and the origins and development over time of new life forms.

Life on Earth began in the ocean. The earliest life forms were single-celled microorganisms. Evidence of these creatures has been found in rocks 3.7 billion years old. Over time, life evolved, generally becoming more complex and varied.

Biologists, anthropologists, and archaeologists research genetics, artifacts, and fossils for clues about how species, including the ancestors of early humans, developed and lived.

Our ancestors split from the common ancestor humans share with chimpanzees more than six million years ago. Scientists have identified about twenty species of early humans, or hominins, who lived before, or in some cases at the same time, as our species: *Homo sapiens*.

All evidence—from DNA analyses, fossils, and archaeological finds—points to one continent and to one idea: modern humans, *Homo sapiens*, evolved about 300,000 years ago in Africa and began migrating from Africa soon after about 200,000 years ago. By about 40,000 years ago, *Homo sapiens* became the only surviving hominin species.

Although researchers have made important discoveries over the years, large pieces of the puzzle are still missing. As paleoanthropologists excavate new areas and use technology, new evidence is unearthed. For example, the discovery in Morocco of *Homo sapiens* bones from 315,000 years ago—farther north and predating earlier specimens—suggests that modern humans could have evolved in different regions of Africa simultaneously.

Each new discovery expands and enriches our understanding of human evolution. As our knowledge grows, new ideas and connections emerge.

Yet questions persist. What species did *Homo sapiens* directly arise from? How will *Homo sapiens* evolve in the future? What will be the next puzzle piece to fall into place?

Timeline of Key Species and Developments in Early Human Evolution

6 to 7 million years ago

Sahelanthropus tchadensis—first discovered in 2001—is one of the earliest known species with humanlike characteristics. This species walked upright on two legs, which aided survival in Central African forests and grasslands.

3.9 to 2.9 million years ago

Australopithecus afarensis lived in East Africa. The most complete

Australopithecus afarensis fossil—the skeleton of a small female whom paleontologists nicknamed "Lucy"—was unearthed in 1974 in Ethiopia. Scientists later discovered evidence—dating back 3.4 million years—that although this species had a largely plant-based diet, they also occasionally ate meat and made stone tools.

1.89 million to 110,000 years ago
Homo erectus is the first hominin to spread beyond Africa, inhabiting northern, eastern, and southern Africa, and western and eastern Asia. First discovered in 1891, early African *Homo erectus* fossils show that these are the oldest known early humans with modern humanlike body proportions suited for walking and running rather than climbing.

700,000 to 200,000 years ago
Homo heidelbergensis, a species which used fire and wooden spears, inhabited Africa, Europe, and possibly Asia. Discovered in 1908, this species was the first known to build shelters, to hunt large animals, and to live in colder climates.

400,000 to 40,000 years ago
Homo neanderthalensis, one of our closest extinct human relatives, inhabited Europe and parts of Asia. First discovered in 1829, the species made and used clothing, sophisticated tools, and symbolic and ornamental objects. They controlled fire, lived in shelters, hunted large animals, ate plant foods, and buried their dead in graves, occasionally marked with offerings such as flowers.

300,000 years ago to the present
Homo sapiens, modern humans, evolved in Africa. The species began migrating from Africa after about 200,000 years ago, arriving first in Asia, and last in the Americas. Within the past 12,000 years, agriculture originated at different times in various parts of the world, leading to the development and growth of villages, towns, and cities.

To Caresse and Jeffery: you are *my* pride. —*CBW*

To Abby Bolden —*EBL*

Acknowledgments

For her careful review of the text and illustrations, the publisher thanks Briana Pobiner, PhD, paleoanthropologist in the Human Origins Program of the Smithsonian's National Museum of Natural History. The publisher is also grateful to the Smithsonian National Museum of Natural History's Human Origins Program for the resources on their website, especially the "Human Family Tree" pages, which can be found at humanorigins.si.edu/evidence/human-family-tree.

Astra Young Readers
An imprint of Astra Books for Young Readers,
a division of Astra Publishing House
astrapublishinghouse.com
Printed in China

ISBN: 978-1-63592-387-2 (hc)
ISBN: 978-1-63592-605-7 (eBook)
Library of Congress Control Number: 2021925837

First edition
10 9 8 7 6 5 4 3 2 1

Design by Barbara Grzeslo
The text is set in Neutraface Demi.
The art is done in watercolor on hot press paper.